BCPL J DELA
Delaunois, Angele.
Magic little words /

DISCARD

OCT 1 9 2015

Broome County Public Library
185 Court Street
Binghamton, NY 13901
607-778-6400
www.bclibrary.info

P9-BZQ-949

Magic Little Words

Text by Angèle Delaunois | Art by Manon Gauthier

Owlkids Books

Good morning

I smile at a
brand-new day.

good
morning

Welcome

I open my heart
and home to you.

I'm sorry

I'm so sad
that I hurt you.

TWEET

Tweet

I love you

The most beautiful song for two.

Rest
in peace

For eyes that have
closed forever.

Bon voyage

I wish you a safe trip
filled with wonder.

Bravo

You did it!
Well done!

Please

A magic key
  that opens most doors.

Thank
you

Little words to
offer like gifts.

Thank you

Good-bye

I miss you already.

Good-bye

Good night

Turn out the lights
and let my dreams begin.

ZZZZ

To Loryck and Liyah—A.D.
For Laura Désirée and Marco—M.G.

Text © 2013 Angèle Delaunois
Illustrations © 2013 Manon Gauthier
English translation © 2015 Owlkids Books

Published in North America in 2015 by Owlkids Books Inc.

Originally published as *Les mots magiques* in 2013 by Éditions de l'Isatis

All rights reserved. No part of this publication may be reproduced, stored in a retrieval system, or transmitted in any form or by any means, without the prior written permission of Owlkids Books Inc., or in the case of photocopying or other reprographic copying, a license from the Canadian Copyright Licensing Agency (Access Copyright). For an Access Copyright license, visit www.accesscopyright.ca or call toll-free to 1-800-893-5777.

Owlkids Books acknowledges the financial support of the Canada Council for the Arts, the Ontario Arts Council, the Government of Canada through the Canada Book Fund (CBF) and the Government of Ontario through the Ontario Media Development Corporation's Book Initiative for our publishing activities.

Published in Canada by
Owlkids Books Inc.
10 Lower Spadina Avenue
Toronto, ON M5V 2Z2

Published in the United States by
Owlkids Books Inc.
1700 Fourth Street
Berkeley, CA 94710

Library and Archives Canada Cataloguing in Publication

Delaunois, Angèle
[Mots magiques. English]
    Magic little words / written by Angèle Delaunois ; illustrated by Manon Gauthier ; translated by Karen Li.

Translation of: Les mots magiques.
ISBN 978-1-77147-106-0 (bound)

    I. Gauthier, Manon, 1959-, illustrator II. Li, Karen, translator III. Title. IV. Title: Mots magiques. English

PS8557.E433M6713 2014   jC843'.54   C2014-906130-7

Library of Congress Control Number: 2014950140

Designed by: Hélène Meunier

Manufactured in Shenzhen, Guangdong, China, in October 2014, by WKT Co. Ltd.
Job #14CB1888

A   B   C   D   E   F

Publisher of Chirp, chickaDEE and OWL
www.owlkidsbooks.com